A NOTE TO PARENTS

Dear Parents,

Every day we measure time or distance, look for patterns, estimate, and count. Whether we realize it or not, we are constantly thinking mathematically.

Children are given a great deal of encouragement when they are learning to count—but the support needn't stop there. Young children love puzzles and riddles, and they eagerly approach problem-solving situations as if they were games. They often see and use a variety of strategies. These are important skills in developing mathematical thinking.

We truly have the power to nurture in our children a long-lasting love for math. We can do this by making a "math connection" to familiar experiences and by supporting our children's natural affinity for the discipline. **Step into Reading Plus Math** books can help. Each book combines an age-appropriate math element with an enjoyable reading experience.

Remember—math is not an isolated phenomenon but is woven into the fabric of our lives. The love of math is a lifelong journey. Celebrate that journey with your child!

Sincerely,

Colleen DeFoyd

Colleen DeFoyd
Primary Grades Math Teacher
Scottsdale, Arizona

To Sam and Cassie
—S.A.

For Meghan, with love
—J.M.

Text copyright © 1998 by Sarah Albee.
Illustrations copyright © 1998 by John Manders. All rights reserved under
International and Pan-American Copyright Conventions. Published in the United
States by Random House, Inc., New York, and simultaneously in Canada by
Random House of Canada Limited, Toronto.
www.randomhouse.com/kids/

Library of Congress Cataloging-in-Publication Data:
The dragon's scales / by Sarah Albee ; illustrated by John Manders.
p. cm. – (Step into reading + math. Step 2 book.)
SUMMARY: When a dragon threatens to disrupt the life of the townspeople, a little
girl challenges the scaly creature to a math contest involving knowledge of weight.
ISBN 0-679-88381-9 (pbk.) — ISBN 0-679-98381-3 (lib. bdg.)
[1. Dragons—Fiction. 2. Weights and measures—Fiction. 3. Contests—Fiction.]
I. Manders, John, ill. II. Title. III. Series. PZ7.A3174Dr 1998
[E]–dc21 97-40337

Printed in the United States of America 10 9 8 7 6 5 4 3 2 1

STEP INTO READING is a registered trademark of Random House, Inc.

Step into Reading® +Math

The Dragon's Scales

BERRY TOWN

By Sarah Albee
Illustrated by John Manders

A Step 2 Book

Random House 🏠 New York

Once there was a small town

beside a wide river.

The town was called Berry Town.

Everyone who lived there

was crazy about berries.

They loved to eat berries.

They loved to look at berries.

They even loved to smell berries.

In the spring, the people

of Berry Town went over the bridge,

across the river, and to the fields.

There they planted all kinds of berries—

strawberries, blueberries, blackberries,

raspberries, and even huckleberries.

In the summer,

when the berries were ripe,

there was a big parade.

Everyone marched

through the town

on their way to the berry fields.

But one year,

when the people of Berry Town

reached the bridge,

something was wrong.

That something
was very big,
very scaly,
and *very* scary.

It was a dragon!

"No one may cross this bridge,"

the dragon said.

"The berries are all mine!"

The townspeople
sadly turned away.
They wanted the berries.
But what could they do?

The dragon was bigger
and stronger and scarier
than any of them.
"Wait!" came a small voice.
It was a little girl named Holly.

"I have an idea,"

Holly said to the dragon.

"Let's have a contest.

If I win, you have to go away."

"Okay," said the dragon.

"But if *I* win, then everyone

has to work in the berry fields for me."

"Is that okay?" Holly asked.

The people of Berry Town nodded.

It was their only chance.

The schoolteacher stepped forward.

"I see that you have a set of scales,"

he said to the dragon.

19

"I will ask three questions about weights,"
said the teacher.

"Whoever gets two out of three
questions right wins.
The dragon's scales
will decide who is right."
"Okay," said Holly.

The dragon was not used

to this kind of contest.

But he knew that

whoever is biggest

and strongest

and scariest *always* wins.

So he nodded.

The dragon gave his scales

to the teacher.

Then the dragon and Holly

stood back to back.

They took one, two,

three steps.

"Which weighs more," asked the teacher, "one apple or two peas?"

The dragon snorted.

"Everyone knows that two things

weigh more than one thing," he said.

"So two peas weigh more than one apple."

"Two things don't always weigh
more than one thing," said Holly.
"What matters is how heavy
the things are.
I know that an apple
is heavier than two peas."

"Let's see who's right,"
said the teacher.

The teacher put the apple

on one side of the scales.

He put the peas on the other.

The apple side went down.

The peas side went up.

The apple weighed more

than the peas!

The townspeople cheered.

The dragon snarled.

Holly and the teacher smiled.

"Next question," said the teacher.
"Which weighs more,
 a little bag of gold
 or a big bag of cotton?"

"Big things weigh more
     than little things," said the dragon.
"So the big bag of cotton *must* weigh
     more than the little bag of gold."

"Just because one thing is bigger
than another doesn't mean
it is heavier," said Holly.
"I know that even a big bag of cotton
is lighter than a little bag of gold."

"Who is right *this* time?"

said the teacher.

The teacher put the bag of gold
on one side of the scales.
He put the bag of cotton on the other.

The gold side went down.

The cotton side went up.

The gold weighed more
than the cotton!

"Time for you to pack up,"

said Holly to the dragon.

The dragon started
to cry.

Holly felt sorry for the dragon.

"I'll ask you one more question,"

she said.

"If you answer it right,

then you can stay.

But you have to promise to be nice."

The dragon sniffled.

"I really *am* nice," he said.

"But no one ever wants
to share with a dragon."

"Which weighs more," Holly asked,
"a bucket of bricks or a bucket of
feathers?"
"The buckets are the same size,"
said the dragon.
"Two things that are the same—"
"Think *very* carefully," said Holly.

The dragon took a deep breath.

He thought very carefully.

"Bricks are heavier

than feathers," he said.

"So even though there is

the same amount of

bricks and feathers,

the bucket of bricks must weigh more."

Holly put the bucket of feathers
on one side of the scales.

She put the bucket of bricks
on the other.

The brick side went down.

The feather side went up.

The bricks weighed more

than the feathers!

The dragon was right!
And that's the story of how
Berry Town got its very own
watchdragon!